For Toad, the dog with
the itchy back
~D.B.

For Bentley, our very
own shaggy dog
~G.W.

This edition produced 2005 for
BOOKS ARE FUN LTD
1680 Hwy 1 North, Fairfield, Iowa, IA 52556
by LITTLE TIGER PRESS
An imprint of Magi Publications
1 The Coda Centre, 189 Munster Road, London SW6 6AW
www.littletigerpress.com

Originally published in Great Britain 2001
by Little Tiger Press, London

Text copyright © David Bedford 2001
Illustrations copyright © Gwyneth Williamson 2001

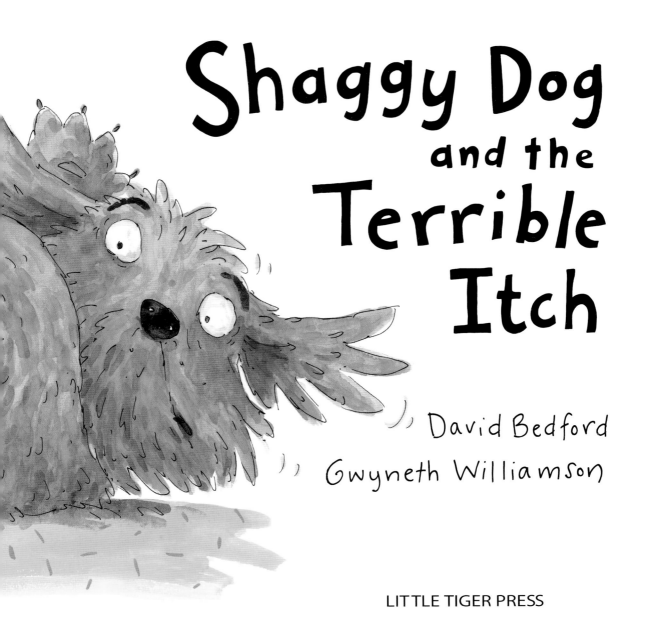

Shaggy Dog
and the
Terrible
Itch

David Bedford

Gwyneth Williamson

LITTLE TIGER PRESS

Shaggy Dog had an itch on his back.
He scratched against a tree but . . .

his back was still itchy.

"Will you scratch my back?"
Shaggy Dog asked Mimi the poodle.
"Ugh!" said Mimi. "Scratch your
back, *no thank you*! I'm off to
the Poodle Parlor for
a wash and trim."

"*I* will scratch your back," said Farmer Gertie. "But first you must help me round up my sheep."

The sheep were hiding, and it took
ages to find them.
"*Woof woof!*" barked Shaggy Dog.
"Come here, sheep, come here *now*!"

At last the sheep were locked in their pen.
Farmer Gertie used her curly crook to scratch
Shaggy Dog's back.
"Ooh!" said Shaggy Dog. "That's much better."
But as Shaggy Dog walked into town . . .

the itch came back!

Shaggy Dog knocked on the window of Merv's Café.

"Who will scratch the itch from
my back?" he asked.
"*I* will," said Merv. "But first you
must wash my pots and pans."

Shaggy Dog washed towers
and towers of pots and pans.
Bubbles covered his legs and
got into his mouth, and when
he had finished, his paws
were all wrinkly.

Merv used a long fork to
scratch Shaggy Dog's back.
"Ooh, ooh!" said Shaggy Dog.
"That's much, much better."
But when Shaggy Dog left
the café . . .

the itch came back!

Shaggy Dog stopped into
Mary Lou's Poodle Parlor.

"Will you scratch the itch from my back?"
asked Shaggy Dog.
"Okay," said Mary Lou. "But only if you
sweep up the fur on the floor."

Shaggy Dog swept up
mountains and mountains
of poodle fur.

Fur got up his nose, and when he
had finished, he had fur in his ears
and his eyes, too.

Achoo!
Achoo!
Achoo!

he sneezed.

Shaggy Dog shook out all the fur,
and Mary Lou used the poodle
brush to scratch his back.
"Ooh, ooh, ooh!" said Shaggy Dog.
"That's much, much, MUCH better."
But when Mary Lou stopped
scratching . . .

*the itch
came back!*

"What can I do?" asked
Shaggy Dog.
"Sit in the chair," said
Mary Lou. "I'll give
you a wash and
trim."

The bubbly shampoo soothed
Shaggy Dog's back.
"Ooh, ooh, ooh, OOOH!" said
Shaggy Dog.

The
poodle scissors
tickled and went

Snip! Snip! Snip!

"Hee, hee, hee,"
giggled Shaggy
Dog.

When Mary Lou had
finished trimming
Shaggy Dog's fur . . .

Shaggy Dog felt

Wonderful!

The itch had gone at last . . .

but where did it go?

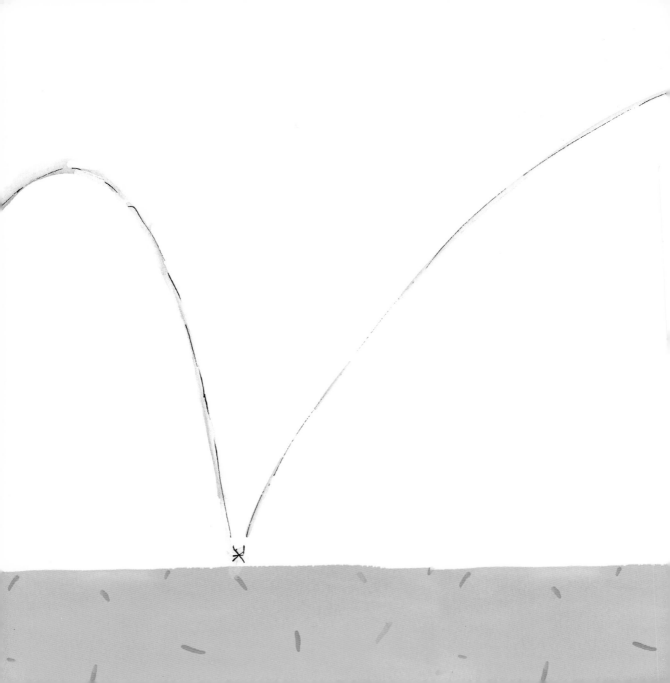